T0380906

MAJOR GRUMPY MORNING MAN

GETTING READY FOR WORK

Jason Gobby

ISBN: Softcover   978-1-7960-0189-1
         EBook   978-1-7960-0188-4

Print information available on the last page

Rev. date: 03/23/2019

To order additional copies of this book, contact:
Xlibris
1-800-455-039
www.xlibris.com.au
Orders@Xlibris.com.au

MAJOR GRUMPY
MORNING MAN

It's 5:30 a.m. when his alarm goes off. Major Grumpy Morning Man washes his face in the trough.

He pulls down his shirt as he pulls up his socks; then he walks to the bathroom and brushes his locks.

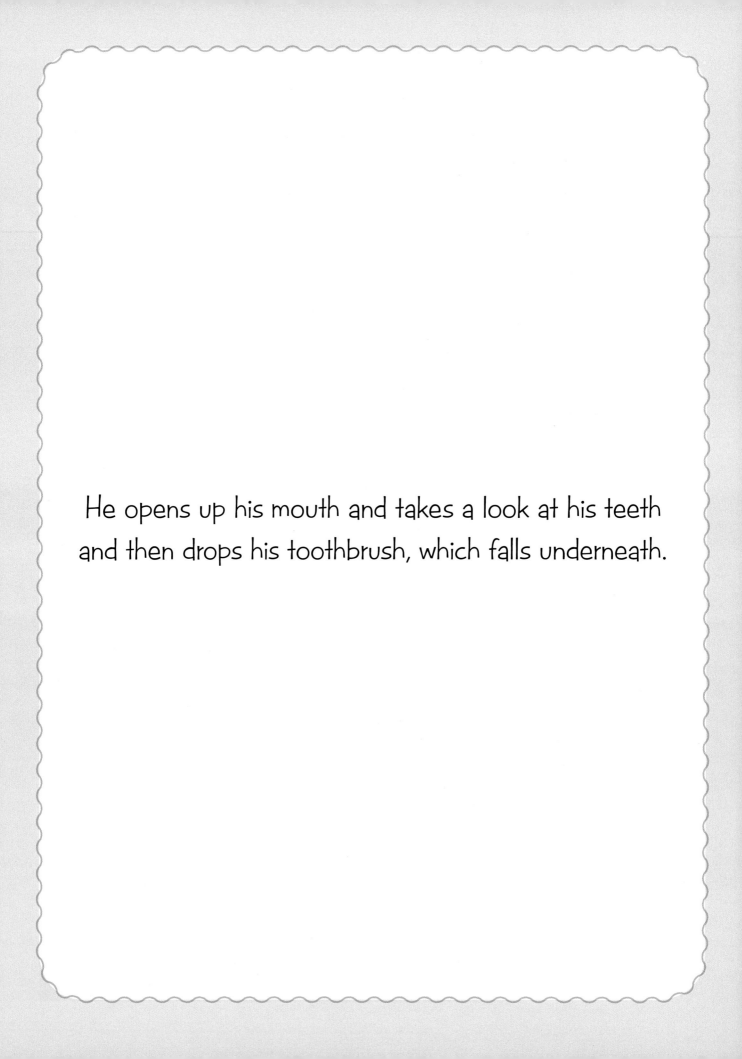

He opens up his mouth and takes a look at his teeth
and then drops his toothbrush, which falls underneath.

Well, he screams, he yells, he jumps, he shouts
Major Grumpy Morning Man lets it all out.

His beautiful wife walks through the door to find
Major Grumpy Morning Man down on the floor,

retrieving his toothbrush that fell underneath
whilst he was trying to brush his teeth.

She's come in to see what the fuss is about
and to tell him to quietly figure it out.

He sits at the table with his juice and his Wheaties. He turns to his wife and says, "Thank you, sweetie."

She says, "No worries," on her way to the shower.

He looks at the clock; he's only got half an hour to get to work, and he can't be late. And at that moment he knocks over his plate.

Well, he screams, he yells, he jumps, he shouts
Major Grumpy Morning Man lets it all out.

His beautiful wife walks through the door to find
Major Grumpy Morning Man down on the floor.

He's wiping up Wheaties that fell from his plate
because he was rushing so he wouldn't be late.

She's come in to see what the fuss is about
and to tell him to quietly figure it out.

He's no longer inside going berserk; he's now in his shed, getting ready for work.

He loads all the tools he needs in his ute. He checks the car's fluids; all levels are beaut.

He walks to the garden and gathers the hose; the tap fitting pops off, and it wets all his clothes.

Well, he screams, he yells, he jumps, he shouts
Major Grumpy Morning Man lets it all out.

His beautiful wife walks out the front door to find
Major Grumpy Morning Man down on the floor.

He's retrieving the fitting that fell off the hose
that eventually went on to wet all his clothes.

She's come out to see what the fuss is about
and to tell him that he is stressing her out.

So pick yourself up off the floor and march yourself through that shed door.

Climb in your ute, and steer round the bend.
Thank you, little ones and all other friends.

Thank goodness he's gone, and that is the end.

Printed in the United States
By Bookmasters